A Sunshine Storybook™

TIGER'S SPECIAL DAY

ILLUSTRATED BY RUTH MOREHEAD
TEXT ADAPTED BY GWEN MONTGOMERY

Modern Publishing
A Division of Unisystems, Inc.
New York, New York 10022

Wake up Rusty! Wake up Tiger! The alarm clock is ringing and it's time to start a new day!

Rusty jumped out of bed and went to brush his teeth. But Tiger didn't move. He didn't feel like getting up, so he stayed right where he was!

"It's a horrible day," grumbled Tiger, when he finally got up. "I don't feel like brushing my teeth."

Then Tiger decided to get something to eat. "I'm awfully hungry, but I don't feel like doing anything today. I don't even feel like pouring the milk." Tiger just stuck his head right into the milk can.

"Help!" cried Tiger. "Help me Rusty, I'm stuck!" Rusty ran to help Tiger. Rusty pulled from the bottom and Tiger wiggled from the top.

Pop! Tiger flew out of the milk bottle and hit the table. A vase of flowers tipped over. The water splashed all over Tiger.

"Well," laughed Rusty, drying off Tiger with a big fluffy towel. "I don't think you're having a very good day," said Rusty.

Rusty put a bowl on the kitchen table.
"Now, let's fix breakfast the right way. And
no more drinking from the bottle."

"You're right!" said Tiger and he poured
the milk carefully into the bowl.

After breakfast, Rusty asked Tiger if
he wanted to play table tennis. "It's your
favorite game. It might cheer you up."
"I've been practicing," said Tiger.
"I'm sure I can beat you now."

Tiger played as hard as he could, but Rusty won the game. "This is a horrible day!" he cried. "Nothing is going right!"

"Well," said Rusty. "Let's go into town. You always like to do that. Look! Mrs. Chipmunk is having a sale. Why don't you make a list of all the things you want?"

"What a great idea!" Tiger cried. "I'll
make my list up right away!" When
Tiger was ready, they went out the door.

"I feel much better now," said Tiger.
"It's a beautiful day. And a walk into
town is just what I need." Rusty and
Tiger laughed and played all the way to
Mrs. Chipmunk's store.

When they came back from the store, Rusty and Tiger put everything away. "Oh! I almost forgot," said Rusty. "I have a present for you, Tiger." And Rusty took out a pretty box wrapped in ribbon.

Tiger unwrapped the present, "I love surprises," he cried. "But oh no, it's a bone!"

"A bone!" cried Rusty. "That's not the surprise I brought for you! Mrs. Chipmunk must have wrapped up the wrong thing!"

"No, she didn't," laughed Tiger.
"That's the surprise I brought for you.
You helped to make this a fun day after
all." Tiger gave Rusty the bone, and
Rusty gave Tiger the toy fish. And
they spent the rest of the day playing
happily together.